# EMIL
## AND THE
# GREAT
# ESCAPE

# ASTRID LINDGREN

# EMIL AND THE GREAT ESCAPE

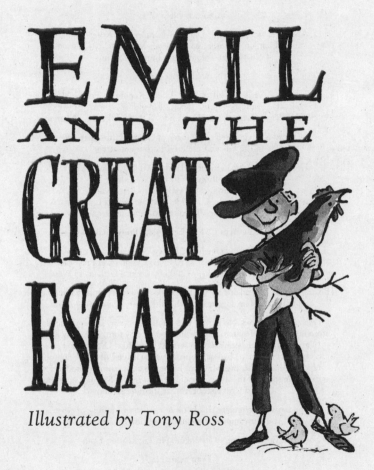

*Illustrated by Tony Ross*

## OXFORD
UNIVERSITY PRESS

# OXFORD
UNIVERSITY PRESS

Great Clarendon Street, Oxford OX2 6DP

Oxford University Press is a department of the University of Oxford.
It furthers the University's objective of excellence in research, scholarship,
and education by publishing worldwide in

Oxford   New York

Auckland   Cape Town   Dar es Salaam   Hong Kong   Karachi
Kuala Lumpur   Madrid   Melbourne   Mexico City   Nairobi
New Delhi   Shanghai   Taipei   Toronto

With offices in

Argentina   Austria   Brazil   Chile   Czech Republic   France   Greece
Guatemala   Hungary   Italy   Japan   Poland   Portugal   Singapore
South Korea   Switzerland   Thailand   Turkey   Ukraine   Vietnam

Oxford is a registered trade mark of Oxford University Press
in the UK and in certain other countries

First published as *Emil i Lönneberga*, Rabén & Sjögren, Stockholm 1963
First published in English 1970 by Brockhampton Press Ltd
First published in this edition 2008 by Oxford University Press

This translation of *Emil and the Great Escape* originally published in Swedish
published by arrangement with Saltkråkan Förvaltning AB

British Library Cataloguing in Publication Data

Data available
ISBN: 978-0-19-272720-6

25 24 23 22

Printed in India by Replika Press Pvt. Ltd.

Paper used in the production of this book is a natural,
recyclable product made from wood grown in sustainable forests.
The manufacturing process conforms to the environmental
regulations of the country of origin.

# Contents

## About Emil

Once upon a time there was a boy called Emil, who lived in Lönneberga. He was a harum-scarum, stubborn little chap, not as nice as *you*, of course, but he *looked* nice enough, that is to say when he wasn't screaming. He had round blue eyes, a round, apple-cheeked face and a mop of fair hair. In fact he often looked so nice that people might have thought he was a perfect little angel. But they would have been quite wrong.

He was five years old and as strong as a young ox, and he lived at Katthult, in Lönneberga, a village in Småland, in Sweden.

One day his father went to town and bought him a cap. Emil was delighted with this cap, and wanted to wear it when he went to bed. His mother wanted to hang it on a peg in the hall, but Emil yelled so that you could have heard him all over Lönneberga. And he slept with his cap on for nearly three weeks. It was one of those with a shiny black peak and a blue crown, and really did feel rather bumpy. But the great thing was that he had got his own way, that was the point.

One Christmas his mother tried to get him to eat some greens, as greens are so good for you, but Emil said no.

'Won't you eat *any* greens?' asked his mother.

'Yes,' said Emil. '*Real* greens.' And he sat quietly down behind the Christmas tree and started chewing it. But he soon tired of that because it scratched his mouth.

Well, that shows how stubborn Emil was. He wanted to boss his father and mother and the entire household, in fact the whole of Lönneberga itself, but the Lönnebergans weren't going to put up with that.

'I pity the folk up at Katthult, having such a badly-behaved boy. They'll never make anything of him,' they said.

Yes, that's what they thought! But they wouldn't have said so if they had known how Emil was going to turn out. Fancy if they had known he was going to be president of the local council when he grew up! You probably don't know what it means to be president of the local council, but I can assure you that it is something very grand, and that's what Emil was going to be, later on.

But just now we will talk about what happened

when Emil was a little boy, living at Katthult in Småland, with his father, whose name was Anton Svensson, and his mother, whose name was Alma Svensson, and his little sister Ida. There was a farm lad, too, called Alfred, and a maidservant called Lina. Because when Emil was a little boy there were servants in Lönneberga and everywhere else. There were farmhands who ploughed and tended the horses and cattle and brought in the hay and planted potatoes, and maidservants who milked and washed up and scrubbed, and sang to the children.

Now you know who lived in Katthult: father Anton, mother Alma, little Ida, Alfred, and Lina. And there were two horses and a pair of oxen, eight cows, three pigs, ten sheep, fifteen hens, a cock, a cat, and a dog. And Emil.

Katthult was a lovely little farmstead, with a red-painted house on a hill and apple trees and lilac bushes all round it. And fields and ploughland and hedges and a lake and a great big wood.

It would have been quiet and peaceful in Katthult, but for Emil.

'He's always getting into mischief, that boy,' said Lina. 'And if he doesn't get into mischief on his own, something's always happening to him. I've never seen such a child.'

But Emil's mother stuck up for him.

'He's not so bad,' she said. 'Today he's only pinched Ida and spilt the cream for the coffee, that's all . . . oh yes, and chased the cat round the

henhouse. I think he's beginning to behave better and growing less wild.'

And he wasn't really bad, nobody could call him that. He was very fond of Ida and the cat. But he had to pinch Ida to make her give him her bread and jam, and he chased the cat just in fun to see if he could run as fast as it could. Although the cat didn't realize this, of course.

It was on the seventh of March that Emil was so good and only pinched Ida and upset the cream and chased the cat. But now you shall hear about three other days in Emil's life, when other things happened, either because he got up to mischief, as Lina said, or because things always happened, wherever Emil was. We can begin with:

**Tuesday the twenty-second of May
when Emil got his head stuck in the soup tureen**

That day they were having meat broth for dinner in Katthult. Lina had served it up in the flowered soup tureen and they were all sitting round the kitchen table eating soup—especially Emil. He liked soup; you could hear that when he ate it.

'Must you make that noise?' asked his mother.

'Well, you can't tell you're having soup, other-wise,' said Emil.

Everyone had as much as they wanted, and the tureen was empty except for a tiny little drop left at the bottom. But Emil wanted that little drop, and the only way he could get it was by pushing his head into the tureen and sucking it up. And that is just what he did. But just fancy! When he tried to get his head out again he *couldn't*! He was stuck fast. It frightened him and he jumped up from the table and stood there with the tureen like a tub on his head. It came right down over his eyes and ears. He hit at it and screamed. Lina was very upset.

'Our lovely soup tureen,' she said. 'Our lovely bowl with the flowers on it. Whatever shall we put the soup in now?'

Because although she wasn't very bright, she did realize that while Emil was in the tureen it would be impossible to serve soup in it.

Emil's mother, however, was more worried about Emil.

'Dear sake's alive, how shall we get the child out? We'll have to get the poker and break the bowl.'

'Have you taken leave of your senses?' asked Emil's father. 'That bowl cost four kronor!'

'Let me have a try,' said Alfred, who was a strong, hefty farmhand. He took hold of both handles and lifted the tureen high up in the air—but what good was that? Emil went with it. Because he was stuck really tight. And there he hung, kicking, trying to get back on the ground again.

'Let go! Let me get down! Let go, I tell you!' he yelled. So Alfred did let go.

Now everybody was very upset. They stood in the kitchen in a ring round Emil, wondering what to do, father Anton, mother Alma, little Ida, Alfred, and

Lina. Nobody could think of a good way of getting Emil out of the soup tureen.

'Look, Emil's crying!' said little Ida, pointing at two big tears sliding down Emil's cheeks from under the edge of the tureen.

'No I'm not,' said Emil. 'It's soup.'

He sounded as cocky as ever, but it isn't much fun being stuck inside a soup tureen—and supposing he never managed to get out! Poor Emil, when would he be able to wear his cap then?

Emil's mother was in great distress about her little boy. She wanted to take the poker and break the tureen, but his father said, 'Not on any account! That bowl cost four kronor. We had better go to the doctor in Mariannelund. He'll be able to get it off. He'll only charge three kronor, and we'll save a krona that way.'

Emil's mother thought that a good idea. It isn't every day that one can save a whole krona. Think of all the nice things you could buy with that, perhaps something for little Ida, who would have to stay at home while Emil was out enjoying the trip.

Now all was hurry and bustle in Katthult. Emil must be made tidy, he must be washed and dressed in his best clothes. He couldn't have his hair combed, of course, and nobody could wash his ears, although they certainly needed washing. His mother did try to get her finger under the rim of the soup tureen so as to get at one of Emil's ears, but that wasn't much use for she, too, got stuck in the bowl.

'There now!' said little Ida, and father Anton got really angry, though as a rule he was very good-tempered.

'Does anyone else want to get stuck in the tureen?' he shouted. 'Well, get on with it for goodness' sake, and I'll bring out the big hay wagon and take everyone in the house over to the doctor in Mariannelund.'

But Emil's mother wriggled her finger and managed to get it out. 'You'll have to go without washing your ears, Emil,' she said, blowing her finger.

A pleased smile could be seen under the rim of the tureen, and Emil said, 'That's the first bit of luck I've had from this tureen.'

Alfred had brought the horse and trap to the front steps and Emil now came out to climb into the trap. He was very smart in his striped Sunday suit and black button boots and the soup tureen—of course it did look a trifle unusual, but it was gay and flowery, something like a new fashioned summer hat. The only criticism that might have been made was that it came down rather too far over Emil's eyes.

Then they set off for Mariannelund.

'Be sure to look after little Ida properly while we're away,' called Emil's mother. She sat in the front with Emil's father. Emil and the tureen sat at the back, and Emil had his cap beside him on the seat. Because of course he would need something to put on his head for the journey back home. A good job he remembered that!

'What shall I get ready for supper?' shouted Lina, just as the trap was moving off.

'Anything you like,' called back Emil's mother. 'I've other things to think about just now.'

'Well, I'll make meat broth then,' said Lina. But at that moment she saw something flowery disappearing round the corner of the road and remembered what had happened. She turned sadly back to Alfred and little Ida.

'It'll have to be black pudding and pork, instead,' she said.

Emil had been several times to Mariannelund. He used to like sitting high up in the trap, watching the winding road and looking at the farms they passed on the way, and the children who lived in them, and the dogs that barked at the gates, and the horses and cows grazing in the meadows. But now it was hardly any fun at all. He sat with a soup tureen over his eyes and could only see a little bit of his own button boots from under the tightly fitting rim of the tureen. He had to keep on asking his father, 'Where are we now? Have we got to the pancake place yet? Are we nearly at the pig place?'

Emil had got his own names for all the farms along the road. The pancake place was so-called because of two small, fat children who had once stood by the gate eating pancakes as Emil went past. And the pig place owed its name to a jolly little pig whose back Emil would scratch sometimes.

But now he sat gloomily looking down at his own button boots, unable to see either pancakes or jolly little pigs. Small wonder that he kept whining, 'Where are we now? Are we nearly at Mariannelund?'

The doctor's waiting-room was full of people when Emil and the tureen went striding in. Everybody there was very sorry for him. They realized that an accident had happened. All except one horrid old man who laughed like anything, just as though there was something funny about being stuck in a soup tureen.

'Haha! Haha!' said the old man. 'Are your ears cold, my boy?'

'No,' said Emil.

'Well, why are you wearing that contraption, then?' asked the old man.

'Because otherwise my ears *would* be cold,' said Emil. He too could be funny if he liked, although he was so young.

Then it was his turn to go in and see the doctor, and the doctor didn't laugh at him.

He just said, 'Good morning! What are you doing in there?'

Emil couldn't see the doctor, but in spite of that of course he had to greet him, so he bowed as low as he could, tureen and all. *Crash!* went the tureen, and there it lay, broken in two. For Emil's head had banged against the doctor's desk.

'There goes four kronor up in smoke,' said Emil's

father to his mother, in a low voice. But the doctor heard him.

'Yes, it's saved you a krona,' he said. 'Because I generally charge five kronor for getting small boys out of soup tureens, and he's managed to do it all by himself.'

Emil's father was pleased and grateful to Emil for having saved a krona. He hurriedly picked up the broken bowl and off he went with Emil and Emil's mother.

When they came out into the street, Emil's mother said, 'Fancy! We've saved a krona *again*! What shall we buy with it?'

'Nothing. We'll save it,' said Emil's father. 'But it is only fair that Emil should have five öre to put in his money-box when we get home.'

And he took a five-öre piece out of his purse straight away and gave it to Emil. You can imagine how pleased Emil was.

So they set off for home. Emil sat in the back seat, delighted with the five-öre piece in his hand

and the cap on his head, as he looked at the children and dogs and horses and pigs as they went past. Had Emil been an ordinary youngster nothing more would have happened that day. But he wasn't! So guess what he did? He put the five-öre bit in his mouth, and just as they passed the pig place, a little 'plop' was heard from the back seat. Emil had swallowed the five öre.

'Oh!' said Emil. 'It *did* go down quick!'

Now there were renewed wails from Emil's mother.

'Dear sake's alive, how are we to get the five öre out of the child? We'll have to go back to the doctor.'

'How well you work things out,' said Emil's father. 'Shall we pay the doctor five kronor so as to get back five öre? Where were you in arithmetic class when you were at school?'

Emil took the matter calmly. He patted his stomach and said, 'I can be my own money-box and have a five-öre piece in my tummy just as well as in my money-box. Because it's no good trying to get anything out of that. I tried with a kitchen knife, so I know.'

But Emil's mother wouldn't give way. She wanted to go back to the doctor with Emil.

'I didn't say anything that time he swallowed those trouser buttons,' she reminded Emil's father. 'But a five-öre piece is much harder metal, believe me; it might be very dangerous.'

And she managed to scare Emil's father so much that he turned the horse and drove back to Mariannelund. Because he, too, was anxious about his boy.

They went rushing breathlessly into the doctor's surgery.

'Have you forgotten something?' asked the doctor.

'No, it's that Emil has swallowed a five-öre bit,' said Emil's father. 'So if you would perform a small operation on him for four kronor, say . . . the five öre could go towards the cost.'

But Emil tugged at his father's coat and whispered, 'None of that—it's mine!'

And the doctor had no intention of taking Emil's five öre away from him. There was no need for an operation, he said. The coin would turn up all right in a couple of days.

'But you should eat five buns,' said the doctor to Emil. 'So that the five öre can have a bit of company and not scratch your stomach.'

He was a delightful doctor, and he didn't charge anything, either. Emil's father was so pleased that he beamed when they went out again.

Emil's mother wanted to go straight away to buy buns for Emil at the Miss Anderssons' Home Bakery.

'No need for that,' said Emil's father. 'We've got buns at home.'

Emil thought for a moment. He was clever at

working things out and he was hungry, too, so he said, 'I've got five öre inside me and if I could get at it I would buy my own buns.'

He reflected for a little longer, then he said, 'Can't you lend me five öre for a couple of days, Father? You'll get it back, sure as eggs!'

Emil's father agreed, and off they went to the Miss Anderssons' Home Bakery and bought five buns for Emil, splendid buns, round and golden brown, with sugar on them. Emil gobbled them up at a great rate.

'That's the best medicine I've ever had in my life,' said he.

Emil's father had become so pleased and excited all of a sudden that he didn't know what he was doing.

'We've saved lots of money today,' he said, and he bought five öre's worth of peppermint rock for little Ida at home.

Then Emil and his parents went back to Katthult. As soon as Emil's father got inside the door, and before he had even taken off his hat and coat, he stuck the tureen together again. It wasn't difficult, it had only been broken in two pieces.

Lina was so pleased that she jumped for joy and shouted to Alfred, who was unharnessing the horse, 'Now there'll be meat broth again in Katthult!'

That's what she thought; she had forgotten Emil!

That evening Emil played longer than usual with little Ida. He built a cottage for her among the stones and boulders in the meadow. She thought it great fun. And he only pinched her a little bit each time he wanted some peppermint rock.

Then it began to get dark, and Emil and little Ida thought about going to bed. They went into the kitchen to see if their mother was there, but she wasn't. Nobody was. Only the soup tureen. It stood on the table, all mended and fine. Emil and little Ida stood looking at the wonderful tureen which had been travelling about all day.

'Fancy, all the way to Mariannelund,' said little Ida. And then, 'How did you get your head into the tureen, Emil?'

'It was quite easy,' said Emil. 'I just did this.'

At that moment Emil's mother came into the kitchen. And the first thing she saw was Emil, standing with the tureen on his head. Emil struck at the tureen, little Ida screamed, Emil screamed as well. For now he was stuck fast again, as he had been before.

Then his mother took the poker and whacked the tureen so that it smashed with a noise that could be heard all over Lönneberga. Crash! it went, and flew into a thousand pieces. Bits of it showered all over Emil. Emil's father heard the noise and came rushing indoors.

He stood silent in the kitchen doorway, and saw Emil and the bits of the tureen and the poker Emil's mother was holding. Not a word did Emil's father say. He just turned and went back to the sheepfold.

But two days later he got five öre from Emil, which was some comfort.

Well, that shows you something of the sort of boy Emil was. It was on Tuesday the twenty-second of May that this soup tureen business happened. But perhaps you would like to hear something about:

*Sunday the tenth of June*
*when Emil hoisted little Ida up the flagstaff*

There was to be a party in Katthult on Sunday, the tenth of June. Many people were coming from Lönneberga and other places. For several days Emil's mother had been preparing food.

'It's going to cost a lot,' said Emil's father. 'But then parties do. We mustn't be niggardly. Though perhaps you could make those meat balls a bit smaller.'

'I'm making them exactly right,' said Emil's mother. 'The right size and the right shape and the right brown colour.'

31

And so she did. And she prepared spare ribs of pork and calves' liver and salmagundi and apple pie and smoked eel and stews and puddings and two giant cheesecakes and a special kind of sausage that was so delicious that people willingly drove all the way from Vimmerby and Hultsfred so as to have some.

Emil liked those sausages very much, too.

It was just the right kind of day for a party. The sun shone, the lilacs and apple trees were in bloom, the air was full of birdsong, and Katthult itself was lovely as a dream, standing there on its hill. The garden paths were newly raked, the house was scoured in every corner, the food was all ready, nothing remained to be done. Yes, one thing!

'Oh, we've forgotten to put up the flag,' said Emil's mother.

Emil's father set off at full speed and ran to the flagstaff, Emil and little Ida close behind him. They wanted to see the flag reach the top of the pole.

'I think it's going to be a lovely, happy party

today,' said Emil's mother to Lina, when they were alone in the kitchen.

'Yes, but mightn't it be better to lock up Emil now rather than later on?' suggested Lina.

Emil's mother looked at her reproachfully, but said nothing.

Lina tossed her head and muttered, 'Well, it's all the same as far as I'm concerned. We'll just see what happens.'

'Emil is a dear little boy,' said his mother, very decidedly. Through the kitchen window she could see the dear little boy running about and playing with his little sister. They were both beautiful as little angels, thought Emil's mother, Emil in his striped Sunday suit, with the peaked cap on his curly hair, and Ida in a new red frock with a white sash round her tubby middle.

Emil's mother smiled contentedly. Then she looked anxiously down the road and said, 'I hope Anton's got the flag up by now, for our guests will be here at any moment.'

Everything seemed to be going all right. But, fancy how annoying! Just as Emil's father was on the point of hoisting the flag, Alfred came hurrying from the cowshed, calling, 'The cow's calving! The cow's calving!'

It was the cow Broka, of course, the maddening creature, who had to calve just when everyone was busy and the flag on the point of being hoisted!

Emil's father had to leave everything and rush off to the cowshed. But Emil and little Ida remained standing by the flagstaff.

Ida leaned her head back as far as it would go, and looked at the golden knob at the top of the pole.

'Ooh, how high up,' she said. 'You could see all the way to Mariannelund from there.'

Emil reflected. But not for long.

'We could soon find out,' he said. 'Shall I hoist you up?'

Little Ida laughed. Oh, how kind Emil was and what funny things he always found to do!

'Yes, I want to see Mariannelund,' said little Ida.

'Well, you shall, then,' said Emil, kindly. And he took the hook that fastened the flag and secured it firmly to Ida's sash. Then he took hold of the cord with both hands.

'Up you go!' said Emil.

'Hee hee!' said little Ida.

And up she went, right up to the top of the flagstaff. Then Emil made the cord fast, just as father did, because he didn't want Ida to fall down and hurt herself. And there she hung, as neatly and firmly as could be.

'Can you see Mariannelund?' shouted Emil.

35

'No,' she shouted back, 'only Lönneberga.'

'Pooh—just Lönne-berga . . . well, would you like to come down then?'

'Not yet,' shouted Ida. 'It's fun seeing Lönneberga too. Oh, here come the visitors.'

And come they did. The whole drive was full of traps and horses and soon people began streaming through the gate and making their way slowly up to the house. Grand Mrs Petrell came first. She had come all the way from Vimmerby in a carriage, so as to have some of Mrs Svensson's sausage. She was very smart, with feathers in her hat, and she stuck out back and front.

Mrs Petrell looked about her in delight. Katthult was looking so beautiful in the sunshine, among the apple trees and lilac; everything was so welcoming, yes, and the flag was flying, she saw that although she was a trifle near-sighted.

The flag! Suddenly Mrs Petrell stood still in astonishment. What on earth had got into the folk at Katthult?

Emil's father was just coming from the cowshed, and Mrs Petrell called out to him, 'My dear Anton! What is the meaning of this? Why are you flying the Danish colours?'

Emil was standing close by. He didn't know what was meant by the Danish colours. He had no idea that it meant the red and white flag of Denmark, where the Danish people live. But he did know that the red and white at the top of the flagstaff wasn't the Danish colours.

'Hee hee!' said Emil. 'That's only little Ida.'

And little Ida laughed from where she was dangling.'Hee hee, it's only me,' she cried. 'I can see right over Lönneberga.'

Emil's father didn't laugh. He brought little Ida down as fast as he possibly could, and she said, 'Hee hee, I haven't had such fun since Emil dyed me red.'

She meant the time Emil had dipped her in the big basin of whortleberry juice when they were playing Indians, so that she should be red all over, as Red Indians are.

Yes, Emil saw to it that Ida should enjoy herself. But he got no thanks for that—quite the contrary. His father grasped him firmly by the arm and shook him.

'What did I say?' said Lina, when she saw Emil's father taking him off to the toolshed. That was where he used to go after getting up to mischief.

Emil screamed and cried. 'She wanted to see Ma . . . ri . . . anne . . . lu . . . und,' he sobbed.

He thought his father was very unjust. Nobody had ever told him he mustn't show little Ida Mariannelund. And it wasn't his fault that she couldn't see more than Lönneberga.

Emil went on crying. But only until his father had locked the door and gone away. Then he stopped. Actually it was pleasant in the toolshed. There were so many bits of wood and odds and ends of boards to make things out of. Emil used to carve a funny little wooden man every time he was shut in the toolshed after getting up to mischief. He had already done fifty-four and it looked as if there were going to be still more.

'I don't care about that stupid old party,' said Emil. 'Father can hoist the flag himself, if he likes. I'm going to make another old man and I shall be cross and horrid all day.'

Emil knew he would soon be let out. He never had to wait long in the toolshed.

'Just until you have thought over this bit of mischief thoroughly, so that you don't do it again,' his father used to say. And Emil was obliging enough seldom to indulge in the same bit of mischief twice over, but would find a new prank every time.

Now he sat carving his wooden figure, thinking over his exploit with Ida. The figure was soon finished, for he had had plenty of practice, and he didn't go on thinking for long. Then he wanted to get out, but they must have forgotten him while they feasted. He waited and waited, but nobody came, so he began wondering how to get out by himself.

Through the window, perhaps? It shouldn't prove very difficult. It was high up, of course, but it was easy to climb up the pile of boards which lay conveniently against the wall.

He opened the window, meaning to jump out, but then he saw a lot of horrid nettles growing just below. It is painful jumping into a bed of nettles. Emil had done so once, to see what it felt like. Now he knew he didn't want to do it again.

'I'll think of a better way,' he told himself.

If you have ever been to a farm like Katthult you will know what it is like and what nice little groups of houses there are. It makes you want to play hide and seek as soon as you get there. At Katthult not only were there stables and cowsheds and pigsties and henhouses and sheepfolds, but a whole lot of other sheds and little houses besides. There was a smokehouse, where Emil's mother used to smoke her lovely sausage, and a wash-house where Lina washed their dirty clothes, and there were two more little houses, close together. In one was the wood and toolshed, and in the other the mangle and food store.

Emil and Ida used to play hide and seek in the evening among these little houses, but not where the nettles were, of course. And now Emil had to remain where he was just because so many nettles were growing between the toolshed and the food store.

He thought hard. He saw that the window of the food store was open, and he had a bright idea. It ought to be a simple matter to put a plank between the window of the toolshed and that of the food store, and climb across. He was thoroughly tired of the toolshed by now, and besides, he was growing hungry.

He never wasted time when he had a good idea. In a twinkling the plank was in place and Emil started crawling along it. It looked dangerous because the plank was narrow and Emil was heavy.

'If all goes well Ida shall have my jumping-jack, I promise,' said Emil as he crawled along. The plank

creaked alarmingly, and when he saw the nettles below he was scared and started wobbling.

'Help!' yelled Emil, and overbalanced. He was already on the way to the nettlebed but just managed to grip the plank with his legs and scramble back again. After that everything went well and he got over into the food store.

'That was easy,' he said. 'But anyway, Ida shall have my jumping-jack . . . I think . . . some other day . . . if it's broken by then . . . well, I'll see.'

He gave the plank a hefty push that sent it back

into the toolshed, because he liked to do things properly. Then he ran to the door and tried it. It was locked.

'I thought as much,' he said. 'But they'll come and fetch the sausage soon, and then I'll be out in a jiffy.'

He sniffed. There was a nice smell in the food store, for there were plenty of good things there. He looked all round. Up under the roof smoked hams and black puddings hung in long rows, a whole line of them, on a pole, for Emil's father was very fond of black pudding with bacon and white sauce. And there in a corner stood the bread chest full of delicious loaves, beside the cutting-board, with all the yellow cheeses and crocks full of freshly churned butter. Behind the table was the wooden vat full of salted pork, and next to it the big cupboard where Emil's mother had her raspberry juice and pickled cucumber and pear ginger and strawberry jam. But on the middle shelf of the cupboard were her delicious sausages.

Emil liked sausages, very much indeed!

The party at Katthult was now in full swing. The guests had had their coffee and lots of buns. Now they were just sitting waiting to get hungry again so as to start on the spare ribs of pork, and salmagundi and sausage and all the rest of it.

Suddenly, Emil's mother cried, 'Oh! We've forgotten Emil! He's been shut up too long, poor child!'

Emil's father ran off at once to the toolshed and little Ida ran after him.

'Now, Emil, you may come out,' cried his father, flinging open the door. Imagine his astonishment. Emil wasn't there!

'The young scamp must have got out through the window,' said Emil's father. But when he looked out and saw the nettles below all uncrushed and standing up straight, he was worried.

'They haven't been disturbed or trodden on by any human foot, at all events,' he said. Little Ida began to cry. What had happened to Emil? Lina used to sing a dreadfully sad song about a girl who was changed into a white dove and flew up to heaven instead of staying inside the horrid barrel in which she had been nailed up. Emil had been locked up, and who could say whether he had been changed and flown out? Little Ida looked about to see if any dove was visible. But all she saw was a white hen pecking for worms by the toolshed.

She cried, and pointed at the hen.

'Perhaps that's Emil,' she said.

Emil's father didn't think it was. But for safety's sake he went in to Emil's mother and asked if she had noticed that Emil could fly.

No, she hadn't. And now there was a great commotion in Katthult. The party had to wait. Everybody had to go out and hunt for Emil.

'He *must* be in the toolshed,' said his mother, and they all rushed there to have a more thorough search.

But no Emil was in the toolshed, only fifty-five little wooden figures standing on a shelf in a row. Mrs Petrell had never seen so many and wondered who had made them.

'Why, our little Emil,' said his mother, beginning to cry. 'He was such a dear little boy.'

'Oh yes,' said Lina, tossing her head. Then she added, 'We'd better have a look in the food store, perhaps.' That wasn't such a bad suggestion, coming from Lina, and off they all rushed. But no Emil was there!

Little Ida went on crying quietly, without stopping, and when nobody was looking she went up to the

white hen and whispered, 'Don't fly up to heaven, Emil dear. I'll give you heaps of chicken food if only you'll stay here at home.'

But the hen wouldn't promise anything; she just clucked and went away.

How those poor people in Katthult hunted and hunted! In the woodshed, the mangling shed and the stable. No Emil was there! In the cowshed and the pigsty—no Emil! In the sheepfold and the hen-house and the smokehouse and the wash-house . . . no Emil. They peered down the well. No Emil was there, which was a good thing, though by now they were all in tears. And the people who had come to the party whispered to each other. 'He really was a dear little chap . . . not really naughty, I always said.'

'He's probably fallen in the stream,' said Lina.

The stream at Katthult was swift and strong and dangerous; small children might easily drown in it.

'You know he's not allowed to go down there,' said his mother, sternly.

Lina tossed her head. 'That's just why,' she said.

Then they all ran down to the stream. Luckily Emil wasn't there, either, though they all cried harder than ever. And Emil's mother had thought it was going to be such a lovely party!

Now there was nowhere else to look.

'Whatever on earth shall we do?' asked his mother.

'We must have a bit of food, anyhow,' said his father, and this was a good idea, for they had become hungry during all the hunting and upset.

Emil's mother began serving the food at once. She wept a little into the salmagundi as she carried it, but put it on the table together with the calves' liver and spare ribs of pork and cheesecakes and everything else. Mrs Petrell licked her lips. This all looked very promising, though she didn't see any sausage, which rather worried her.

But just at that moment Emil's mother said, 'Lina, we've forgotten the sausage! Run and fetch it.'

Lina ambled off. Everyone waited eagerly, and Mrs Petrell nodded. 'Sausage, yes,' she said, 'that will be very nice at this distressing time.'

Then Lina returned. Without the sausage.

'Come with me and I'll show you something,' she said.

She looked rather odd, but she always did, so that was nothing out of the ordinary.

'What do you mean by this nonsense?' asked Emil's mother sharply.

Lina looked even odder and laughed quietly in a peculiar way.

'Come with me,' she said again, and they all did so.

Lina led the way to the storehouse, and all the time they heard her laughing strangely and quietly to herself. She opened the heavy door and stepped over the high threshold and went up to the big cupboard and opened its door with a crash and pointed to the middle shelf, where Emil's mother kept her delicious sausage.

There was no sausage there now. But—Emil was there!

He was asleep. There he lay, the dear little boy, asleep among all the sausage skin, and his mother was as delighted as if she had found a gold nugget

in her cupboard. What did it matter that he had eaten all the sausage? It was a thousand times better to find *him* on the shelf than two kilos of sausage. Emil's father thought the same.

'Hee hee, there's Emil,' said little Ida. 'He isn't transformed, not much, anyway.'

To think that finding one little boy, full of sausage, could make so many people happy! Now at last, a jolly, splendid party began in Katthult. Emil's mother discovered a little bit of sausage that Emil hadn't managed to eat, and gave it to Mrs Petrell, to her great delight. And the others, who didn't get any sausage, didn't go hungry. There was calves' liver and spare ribs of pork and meat balls and soused herring and salmagundi and stews and puddings and jellied eels as much as they could eat. And to end up with they had the most delectable curd cake with raspberry syrup and whipped cream.

'This is the nicest thing in the world,' said Emil. And if you have ever eaten the sort of curd cake they had in Katthult, you will know that Emil never said a truer word.

Then came evening, with a beautiful sunset over Katthult and the whole of Lönneberga and

Småland. Emil's father hauled down the flag. Emil and little Ida stood watching.

And so ended the party at Katthult. Everybody went home. One trap after another rolled away. Last of all went grand Mrs Petrell in her carriage. Emil and Ida heard the clop clop of horses' hooves die away down the hill.

'I hope she'll be nice to my little rat,' said Emil.

'What rat?' asked Ida.

'The one I put in her handbag,' said Emil.

'*Why* did you?' asked little Ida.

'Because I felt sorry for it,' said Emil. 'It had never seen anything except the sausage cupboard in all its life and I thought it might at least see Vimmerby.'

'I hope Mrs Petrell will be kind to it,' said little Ida.

'She's sure to be,' said Emil.

It was on the tenth of June that Emil hoisted little Ida up the flagpole, and ate all the sausage. Perhaps you'd like to hear something about:

*Sunday the eighth of July*
*when Emil went on a spree on Hultsfred Plain*

Alfred, the farmhand at Katthult, was fond of children. He liked Emil especially and didn't mind his being a scamp and getting up to mischief. He had carved him a fine wooden gun. It looked exactly like a real one, though you couldn't shoot with it of course. But Emil yelled 'BANG! BANG!' and shot with it, anyhow, so that the Katthult sparrows dared not go out for several days. Emil loved his gun and insisted on having it in bed with him at night.

Yes, he loved his gun, and still more he loved

Alfred, who had made it for him. So it wasn't surprising that Emil cried when Alfred went away to Hultsfred Plain for his military training. That's what it is called when men learn to be soldiers. All the farmhands in Lönneberga and everywhere else have to learn to be soldiers.

'And fancy them having to go just when it's haymaking time,' said Emil's father.

He didn't at all like having to do without Alfred during the haymaking, for that was a busy time in Katthult. However, it wasn't Emil's father, but the king and his generals who decided when the farmhands should go to Hultsfred Plain and learn to be soldiers. Besides Alfred would be able to come back home again when he had finished his training, and that wouldn't take very long. So there was no need for Emil to go on crying, but he did cry all the same, and so did Lina. Because Emil wasn't the only one who was fond of Alfred.

Alfred didn't cry. He said one could go on a spree and have great fun in Hultsfred. And when the trap went off with him and they were all standing sadly waving farewell, he grinned and sang and made jokes to cheer them up. This is part of what he sang.

> O Eksjö town is full of girls
> Who love to go a-dancing.
> Hey diddle di-di-di-do.
> And so they do on Hultsfred Plain
> Where pretty Maud and Kate and Jane
> With swinging skirts and bobbing curls
> Sing hey diddle di-di-di-do,
> Their bright eyes gaily glancing.
> Hey di-do, diddle diddle di-do.

That was the last they heard, for Lina started to howl for all she was worth, and the trap disappeared round the corner, carrying Alfred away to his military training.

Emil's mother tried to comfort her.

'Cheer up, Lina,' she said. 'Wait till the eighth of

July when there's a fête on Hultsfred Plain and we'll go and see Alfred then.'

'I want to go on a spree and see Alfred at Hultsfred, too,' said Emil.

'So do I,' said little Ida.

But Emil's mother shook her head. 'It's no place for small children at such a time,' she said. 'They'd get lost in the crowd.'

'I like getting lost in the crowd,' said Emil, but it was no use.

Emil's father and mother and Lina went off to the Hultsfred fête on the morning of the eighth of July, leaving Emil and little Ida at home with Krösa-Maja who was to look after them. She was an old woman who sometimes came to Katthult to lend a hand at various jobs.

Little Ida was a good child. She sat on Krösa-Maja's knee and got her to tell some of her most dreadful ghost stories, which delighted Ida.

Not so Emil. He was absolutely furious, and went out behind the stables, with his gun.

'I won't have it,' he said. 'I'm going to Hultsfred on the spree, like the others, and that's that. Do you understand, Jullan?'

This last remark was addressed to their old mare which was grazing in the meadow behind the stables. They had a young horse, too, at Katthult, named Markus. But at the moment Markus was on the way to Hultsfred, with Emil's father and mother and Lina—yes, some people could go off and enjoy themselves!

'Well, I know two who are soon going after them at top speed,' said Emil. 'And that's you and me, Jullan.'

And that is what happened. Emil put the bridle on the old mare and led her out of the meadow.

'There's nothing to worry about,' he told Jullan. 'Alfred will be pleased when I turn up, and you're sure to find another nice old mare to whinny with, if you're not much good at going on the spree.'

He pushed Jullan up against the gate, so that he could climb on to her back. He was a smart lad, was Emil.

'Off we go,' said Emil. 'Gee-up, gee-up, we'll say goodbye to Krösa-Maja when we get back home.'

So Jullan went cloppeting off down the hill with Emil, and he sat up, straight and cocky, with his gun in front of him—yes, that too had to go to Hultsfred. Because if Alfred was going to be a soldier, Emil thought he himself would be one as well. Alfred had a rifle, Emil had a gun, which was practically the same thing; they were both soldiers, and that was what Emil wanted.

Jullan was old. She didn't go fast when she trotted,

and so that they shouldn't lose headway entirely,
Emil sang to her:

> 'My old grey mare may be knock-kneed,
> But she keeps up a steady speed,
> So I don't care.

> 'I'm carrying a loaded gun,
> So just be careful, everyone,
> Beware! Beware!'

Well, with Jullan plodding and lumbering and cloppeting along, she and Emil did arrive at Hultsfred
Plain at last.

'Hey!' cried Emil. 'Now we can go on a spree!'

But he stopped short and stared, wide-eyed. He
knew well enough that there were lots of people in
the world, but not that the whole lot of them had
crowded on to Hultsfred Plain. He had never seen
so many people! They stood in thousands all round
the great level plain, and right in the middle of it

were soldiers drilling, shouldering arms and turning left and right and doing the things soldiers do. A fat, cross little man was riding round on a horse, shouting and bellowing at the soldiers, telling them what to do, and they let him shout, and did just what he wanted them to. Emil thought this very strange.

'Isn't Alfred in charge of things?' he asked a couple of peasant lads close by. But they just looked at the soldiers and didn't answer.

Emil, too, thought it fun to watch the soldiers shoulder arms, though not for long because, first and foremost, he wanted to find Alfred—that was why he had come. But all the soldiers were wearing blue uniforms and looked alike. It wasn't easy to pick out Alfred in all that crowd.

'Oh well, just wait till Alfred sees me,' said Emil to Jullan. 'He'll come along shouting "Hey there!" and that cross old chap can bash about with the rifle as much as he likes.'

And in order that Alfred should see him, Emil

rode right up in front of all the soldiers and hullooed as hard as he could.

'Where are you, Alfred? Come on, so that we can go on a spree. Can't you see it's me?'

Yes, Alfred saw well enough that Emil was there with his gun and his cap and his old mare. But he stood among the crowd of soldiers not daring to come forward because of the fat, angry little man who shouted and bellowed and kept giving orders the whole time.

Instead, however, the fat little man came riding up to Emil and said very kindly, 'What's the matter, my boy? Have you lost your mummy and daddy?'

It was the silliest thing Emil had heard for a long time.

'*I'm* not lost,' he said. 'I'm *here*! If anyone's lost it's Mother and Father.'

And actually he was perfectly right. His mother had said that small children might get lost on Hultsfred Plain. But now she and Emil's father and

Lina were all in the thickest of the crowd, unable to move in the crush, and all feeling lost.

But they did see Emil, with his cap and gun and the old mare, and his father said, 'That means another wooden doll for Emil.'

'Yes indeed,' said his mother. 'But how are we going to get hold of him?'

Yes, that was the point. If you have ever attended the sort of fête they have on Hultsfred Plain, you will understand what a squash there was. As soon as the soldiers had finished drilling and marched off, the entire place became crammed with people. There was such a turmoil that you could scarcely find yourself, let alone Emil. Not only did Emil's father and mother want to get hold of him, but so did Alfred. Because he was free now and didn't have to train any more. Now he wanted to be with Emil and have some fun. But it was impossible to find anyone in all that crowd. Nearly everybody was going round looking for somebody. Alfred was hunting for Emil, Emil was looking for Alfred, Emil's mother was looking for Emil, Lina was hunting for Alfred, and Emil's father was looking for his mother—yes, she really was lost for a time and Emil's father had to search for nearly two hours before he found her jammed between two big fat men from Vimmerby, and almost in despair.

But Emil found nobody and nobody found Emil. So he realized that he would have to start going on a spree all by himself if he meant to do it at all.

Before he started, though, he must arrange for Jullan to have some nice old mare to whinny with meanwhile, for he had promised her as much.

He didn't find an old mare, but he found Markus, which was much better. Markus was standing fastened to a tree at the edge of the wood, eating hay. And close by was the trap from Katthult. You could see Jullan was glad when she met Markus again. Emil tied her to the same tree and fetched a pile of hay from the trap. Jullan started munching at once, and then Emil realized that he too was hungry.

But I won't eat hay to start with, he told himself.

And he didn't need to, either. There were lots of little stalls where you could buy sandwiches and sausages and buns and cakes galore, if you had the money. And there were heaps of jolly things to do, and see. The circus, the dancing and amusement parks and merry-go-round and other delights . . .

 imagine, there was a sword-swallower who could swallow swords, and a fire eater who could eat fire, and a grand lady with a beard, who couldn't swallow anything except coffee and buns, one at a time. Of course that wouldn't make her rich; it was a good thing she had her beard. She let people see it if they paid for doing so, and she made quite a lot that way.

But everything cost money, and Emil had no money. However, he was a smart little chap as I have already said. He wanted to see as much as he could, and he began with the circus; for that was the easiest. You only had to climb on to a box at the back of the tent and peep through a hole in the canvas. But Emil laughed so much at the funny clown who was running about inside the tent that he fell off the box and banged his head on a stone. That put him off the circus. Besides, he was hungrier than ever.

You can't go on a spree without food, he said to himself, and I can't get food without money. I'll have to think.

He had noticed that people got money by various means in this place, so there must be a way in which he could do so too. He couldn't swallow swords or fire, and he hadn't a beard, so what could he do? He stood still, reflecting.

Then he saw a poor old blind man sitting on a box in the middle of a crowd of people. He was singing the most doleful songs and sounded very melancholy, but he was getting money for it. He had put his hat on the ground beside him, and kind people kept throwing in small coins all the time.

'I can do that, too,' thought Emil, 'and luckily I've got my cap with me.'

He put the cap on the ground in front of him and began singing 'My Old Grey Mare'.

At once people gathered round him. 'Oh, what a dear little boy,' they said. 'He must be very poor as he's singing for money.'

At that time there were a great many poor children who had nothing to eat,  and now a lady came along and said to Emil, 'Have you had anything to eat today, my little friend?'

'Yes, but only hay,' said Emil.

They all felt very sorry for him. A dear little peasant from Vena had tears in his eyes as he looked at the poor little boy standing there all alone, who had such beautiful flaxen hair. They all started throwing two-, five-, and ten-öre bits into Emil's cap. The nice little peasant from Vena drew a two-öre bit out of his pocket, but changed his mind and stuffed it back again, and whispered to Emil, 'If you come with me to my cart you shall have a little more hay.'

But now Emil had his cap full of money and was rich. He went to a stall and bought lots of sandwiches and buns and cakes and fruit drinks.

When he had stuffed himself full of good things he went on the merry-go-round forty-two times for four kronor and twenty öre. He had never been on one before and hadn't known there was anything so jolly in the whole world.

Now I'm on a spree, at all events, he thought, as he whirled round with his hair blowing in the breeze. I've had some fun before, but never anything to touch this.

Then he looked at the sword swallower and the fire eater and the bearded lady, and after this he only had two öre left.

I'll sing some more and get my cap full again, he thought. Everyone here is so nice.

But then he realized he was feeling tired. He didn't want to sing any more and he didn't want any money, so he gave the blind man the two-öre bit. Then he mooched round looking for Alfred.

Emil was mistaken in thinking that *everyone* was nice. There were one or two bad characters who had gone to Hultsfred Plain, that day. At that time a horrible thief was terrorizing the neighbourhood. He was called the Sparrow, and Småland went in fear of him. Many of his exploits figured in the *Småland Times* and the *Hultsfred Post*. Whenever there was a fête or a fair where people and money were to be found, it was pretty certain that the Sparrow would turn up and begin stealing anything he could lay his hands on. He wore different beards and moustaches every day so as not to be recognized.

He had come to Hultsfred Plain that day and was slinking around in a black slouch hat and black moustache. Nobody knew he was the Sparrow, or it would have caused great alarm among them all.

But had the Sparrow been wise he wouldn't have come to Hultsfred Plain that day, when Emil and his gun were there. For guess what happened?

Emil was wandering about looking for Alfred. He came past the bearded lady's tent, and through the opening he saw her sitting inside, counting up her money, for she wanted to see how much she had made out of her beard on that one Sunday. It must have been quite a large amount, for she beamed and stroked her beard, contentedly. Then she saw Emil.

'Come in, little boy,' she said. 'You may look at my beard for nothing because you seem such a nice little chap.'

Emil had, as it happened, seen that beard before, but he wouldn't refuse the invitation, since it was to be gratis. He strode into the tent with his gun and his cap, and looked at the beard to the tune of about twenty-five öres' worth.

'How did you get such a splendid beard?' he asked, politely.

But the bearded lady never managed to reply. Because at that very moment a terrible voice cried, 'Give me the money at once, or I'll cut off your beard!'

It was the Sparrow. He had sneaked inside the tent, unnoticed.

The bearded lady's face turned white, except where the beard was, of course. The poor soul was just going to let the Sparrow have all her money, when Emil whispered, 'Take my gun!' And she took the gun Emil thrust towards her. It was pretty dark inside the tent; one couldn't see very clearly. The lady thought it was a real gun that you could shoot with. And the best of it was . . . that the Sparrow thought so too!

'Hands up, or I fire!' screamed the bearded lady. And then the Sparrow's face turned white and he put up his hands and stood trembling, while the bearded lady yelled for the police so loudly that she could be heard all over Hultsfred Plain.

The police arrived, and that was the last that was seen of the Sparrow in Hultsfred or anywhere else. And that put an end to stealing in Småland. The bearded lady received plenty of praise in the *Småland Times* and *Hultsfred Post* for having caught the Sparrow. But nobody wrote a word about Emil and his gun, so I think it's time people should know the truth.

'It was a lucky thing I took my cap and my gun to Hultsfred,' said Emil, when the police had taken the Sparrow off to the lock-up.

'Yes, you're a clever little chap,' said the lady. 'And you shall have a look at my beard whenever you like, without paying.'

But Emil was tired. He didn't want to look at a beard or go on a spree or anything. He only wanted to go to sleep. Because it was getting dark by now. Fancy, the whole long day had passed without his finding Alfred!

Emil's father and mother and Lina were tired too. They had hunted and hunted for Emil, and Lina had hunted and hunted for Alfred and now none of them could do anything more.

'Oh, my feet!' said Emil's mother, and his father nodded, grimly.

'Yes, that's the fun of a fête like this,' he said. 'Come on, let's get home to Katthult, there's nothing more we can do.'

And they went off to the edge of the wood to harness the horse and get away. Then they saw Jullan tied to the same tree as Markus, eating hay.

Emil's mother burst into tears. 'Oh, where *is* my little Emil?' she said. But Lina tossed her head.

'He's always up to mischief, that boy,' she said. 'He's a proper scamp.'

Then they heard somebody come running up, quite out of breath. It was Alfred.

'Where's Emil?' he asked. 'I've been hunting for him all day.'

'I don't care where he is,' said Lina. She clambered up into the trap to go home. And—fancy! She stepped on Emil!

There was a little hay left in the trap, and in that hay lay Emil, asleep. But he woke up when Lina trod on him. He saw who had just arrived and was standing there in his blue uniform, panting, and he stretched up his arm and put it round Alfred's neck.

'So there you are, Alfred,' he said, and fell asleep again.

Then they went to Katthult. Markus drew the trap and Jullan trotted behind. Emil woke up from time to time and saw the dark wood and the light summer sky and smelt the horses and the evening air and heard the clop of hooves and the grating of the wheels. But for the most part he slept, and dreamed that Alfred would soon come back to Katthult and to him. Which was true.

It was the eighth of July when Emil went on the spree. Guess if anyone else had been looking for him that day? Ask Krösa-Maja! No don't, because she  got a rash on her arms if you did, and it tickled and wouldn't go away.

Now you have heard what Emil did on the twenty-second of May and the tenth of June and eighth of July, but there are lots of other days in the almanack for those who want to get up to mischief—and that's what Emil did. He got up to mischief almost every day of the year, but specially on the nineteenth of August and the eleventh of October and third of November. Ha ha ha! I have to laugh when I think of what he did on the third of November, but I shan't tell you, for I promised his mother I wouldn't. Though it was after that affair that the people of Lönneberga held a committee meeting. They pitied the Katthult folk for having such a rascally boy. So they each contributed fifty öre and brought the money to Emil's mother in a bag.

'Perhaps this will be enough for you to send Emil away to America,' they said.

Well! That would have been a nice thing! Sending Emil off to America . . . who knows what they would have done for a president of the local council then! When the time came, I mean.

Emil's mother would have nothing to do with such a silly suggestion. She was angry and flung down the bag so that the money flew out all over Lönneberga.

'Emil's a dear little fellow,' she cried. 'And we love him just as he is!'

All the same she was a bit troubled about Emil. Mothers are, when people come and complain about their children. And that night, when Emil was in bed with his cap and his gun she went up and sat beside him for a bit.

'Emil,' she said, 'you'll soon be big enough to start school. What's to happen when you are such a nuisance, and get up to so much mischief?'

Emil lay there looking like a little angel, with his round blue eyes and woolly flaxen hair.

'Tra-la-tra-la lalala,' he said, for he didn't want to listen.

'Emil,' said his mother, sternly, 'what do you think will happen when you begin school?'

'Well,' said Emil. 'I suppose I'll have to stop getting into mischief when I start school.'

Emil's mother sighed.

'Well, we'll hope so,' she said, getting up and going towards the door. Then Emil popped his head over the side of the bed and smiled like a little angel, and said, 'But I'm not quite certain.'

# ASTRID LINDGREN

Astrid Lindgren (1907–2002) is one of the most widely-read children's authors in the world. In the course of her life she wrote over 80 books for children, and has sold over 160 million copies worldwide. She once commented, 'I write to amuse the child within me, and can only hope that other children may have some fun that way too'.

Many of Astrid Lindgren's stories are based upon her memories of childhood and they are filled with lively and unconventional characters. Perhaps the best known is *Pippi Longstocking*, first published in Sweden in 1945. It was an immediate success, and was published in England in 1954.

Awards for Astrid Lindgren's writing include the prestigious Hans Christian Andersen Award and the International Book Award. In 1989 a theme park dedicated to her — *Astrid Lindgren Varld* — was opened in her home town of Vimmerby. When she passed away in 2002, the Swedish Government founded The Astrid Lindgren Memorial Award (ALMA) in her honour. It is the world's largest prize for children's and young adult literature.

*You can read more about Emil's hilarious adventures in*
*Emil's Clever Pig. In it, Emil helps extract a bad tooth,*
*becomes a hero, and has a very unusual pet . . .*
*Here is a short extract.*

Cows have to be milked, even on Sundays. At five o'clock in the morning the alarm clock went off in the kitchen and Lina staggered out of bed with the most terrible toothache. She took one look at herself in the mirror and gave a shrill scream. Good heavens, what a sight she was! Her right cheek was swollen up like a big breakfast bun. No, it was too awful. Lina began to cry.

It was a real shame, for this was the very day that nearly the whole village was coming to Katthult for an after-church coffee party.

'I can't possibly let them all see me with one side of my face different from the other,' moaned Lina, and she went off to milk the cows, sniffling.

She hadn't long to worry about one side being different from the other, for no sooner had she seated herself on the milking stool than a wasp came and stung her on the left cheek. You'd think she would have been happy now, for her left cheek swelled up at once and was just the same size as the other one. Now she had what she wanted, for she looked the same on both sides, but she cried harder than ever.

When she came into the kitchen, everyone was sitting at the breakfast table, and I can tell you that their eyes opened wide when the swollen-cheeked, red-eyed creature that was supposed to be Lina suddenly appeared in the doorway. Poor girl, the sight of her was enough to make anyone cry; so it wasn't very nice of Emil to laugh.

He was just going to drink some milk as Lina came in. When he caught sight of her over the top of his glass he snorted so hard that the milk flew right across the table and splattered all over his father's fine Sunday waistcoat. Then Alfred gave a little snigger, too. Emil's mother looked sternly at Emil and Alfred, and said that this was no laughing matter. But while she was wiping the milk off Emil's father's waistcoat, she took another look at Lina and she understood why Emil had snorted—although she really felt sorry for Lina.

'Poor girl,' she said. 'You look awful. You'll have to keep out of the way when the guests come. Emil, you'll have to run over to Krösa-Maja's and ask her to come and help us serve the coffee.'

The Lönneberga people like drinking after-church coffee on Sundays; so on the farms all round everyone had been delighted when a letter came from Emil's mother saying:

*Dear Ladies and Gentlemen,*

*Alma and Anton Svensson of Katthult, Lönneberga, cordially invite you to an after-church coffee party on Sunday.*

Now it was time to go to church. Emil's father and mother set off. Obviously they had to go to church first, before there could *be* any after-church coffee.

Emil went off obediently with the message to

Krösa-Maja. It was a beautiful morning, and he was whistling gaily when he turned on to the path that led to her cabin in the forest.

If you have ever been in a forest in Småland on an early summer morning in June, you know just what it is like. You hear the cuckoo call and the blackbirds whistle, you feel the softness of the path strewn with pine needles under your bare feet and the warmth of the sun on your neck. You walk along smelling the resin from the fir trees and the pine trees, and in the glades you see the white blossoms of the wild strawberries. Emil was enjoying the walk so much that he took a long time to get to Krösa-Maja's, but at last he came to her cabin, which was so small and grey and ramshackle that you hardly noticed it among the pines.

Inside sat Krösa-Maja reading the *Småland's Daily News* and gloating over some horrifying story she had found in it.

'*Typhus* has come to Jönkoping,' she said, before she had even said good morning to Emil, and she pushed the newspaper under his nose so that he could read it himself. Sure enough, it stated that two inhabitants of Jönkoping were seriously ill with typhus, and Krösa-Maja nodded her head delightedly.

'Typhus is a horrible disease,' she said. 'And we'll soon have it here in Lönneberga, mark my words.'

'But why? How can it get here?' asked Emil.

'It's flying all over Småland like dandelion seeds, even while you're standing here,' said Krösa-Maja. 'Pounds and pounds of typhus seeds, and heaven help anyone they settle on.'

'What's it like? Is it like the plague?' asked Emil. Krösa-Maja had told him about the plague. She kept track of all kinds of diseases and epidemics, and she had told him that the plague was a ghastly thing which once upon a time, a long time ago, had killed nearly everybody in Småland. Just think if typhus was as bad as that!

Krösa-Maja thought for a moment.

'Oh yes, it's rather like the plague,' she said with satisfaction. 'I'm not quite sure, but I seem to remember that first you get blue in the face and then you die. Oh yes, typhus is a terrible disease. Oh, dear me yes.'

But then Emil told her about Lina's toothache and how her cheeks were all swollen just when they were going to have an after-church coffee party, so Krösa-Maja promised to come to Katthult as fast as her legs would carry her.

Emil went home and found Lina sitting on the kitchen step moaning about her toothache, with Alfred and little Ida standing by helplessly.

'There's only one thing to do, you'll have to go to Sme-Pelle,' said Alfred.

Sme-Pelle was the smith in Lönneberga, and he was the man who pulled aching teeth with his big fearsome pincers.

'How much does he charge for pulling out a tooth?' asked Lina between sniffles.

'A krona an hour,' said Alfred, and Lina shuddered when she realized how expensive it was *and* how long it might take.

Emil thought hard, and then he said, 'I can get rid of your tooth cheaper and quicker. I know exactly what to do.'

Then he explained to Lina and Alfred and little Ida what he was going to do.

'I only need two things—Lukas and a long piece of cobbler's twine. I'll tie the twine round your tooth, Lina, and I'll tie the other end to the back of my belt. Then I'll gallop off on Lukas and *ploff*—out comes the tooth.'

'*Ploff* indeed. Thanks very much,' said Lina. 'There's going to be no galloping off with me!'

But just then her tooth gave a terrible twinge, and that made her change her mind. She gave a deep sigh.

'All right, we'll try it. Lord protect me, oh, poor me!' she said and went to get some twine.

Then Emil did just what he had said. He led Lukas to the kitchen step, and when he had finished tying both ends of the twine, he mounted Lukas. Poor Lina whimpered and moaned when she stood tied up behind the horse's tail. Little Ida trembled, but Alfred said cheerfully, 'Now all we have to do is wait for the *ploff*!'

Emil set off at a gallop.

'It'll soon come now,' said little Ida.

But it didn't. Because Lina set off at a gallop, too. She was so afraid of the *ploff* that would come as soon as the thread was taut that she bolted forward just as fast as Lukas, in a dreadful panic. Emil yelled at her to stop, but it made no difference. Lina ran, the twine hung slack, and there was no *ploff*.

But Emil had made up his mind to help Lina get rid of her tooth, so he headed for the nearest fence and Lukas sailed over it. Lina followed behind and, terrified out of her wits, she sailed over it too. Little Ida was watching and you can be sure that as long as she lived she never forgot the sight of Lina, with her swollen cheeks and bulging eyes and the twine hanging out of her mouth, leaping over the fence and screaming, 'Stop! Stop! I don't want a *ploff*!'

Afterwards Lina was ashamed of herself because she had spoilt everything, but by then it was too late; so she again sat down on the kitchen step, nursing her tooth and looking miserable. But Emil didn't give up.

'I'll have to think of another way,' he said.

'Yes, but can we have one that's not quite so fast,' begged Lina. 'The nasty tooth doesn't *have* to come out with a *ploff*. You can just as well pull it out slowly.'

And after Emil had thought for a moment, he knew how to go about it.

Lina had to sit down on the ground with her back against the big pear tree and, while Alfred and Ida looked on curiously, Emil tied her tightly to the trunk with a strong rope.

'Now see if you can run,' he said. Then he picked up the twine which was still hanging out of Lina's mouth and went with it to the grindstone that Alfred used to sharpen his scythe and Emil's father used to sharpen his axes and knives. He tied the twine to the handle, and then all he had to do was to turn the handle . . .